A Day O

Written and illustrated by Petr Horáček

Collins

The granny is sleeping. The cat is looking
at the bird. Look! The bird can get out!
It is time for the bird to fly.

The cat jumps up. The bird jumps off his perch. Look out! He flies out into the room. He must get away.

The bird flies out of the window, out of
the room, out of the house. Just in time.
The bird is out. The bird is free.

It is windy, but the sun is out. It is fun to fly. But look out ... What is it? It is a dog. A big dog!

The bird hides in the bird stand. He likes
it in there. It is safe, no one can get him
in the bird stand.

But look out! The dog can see the bird. The bird stand is too small for the two of them. The bird flies out. Just in time.

The bird flies past the farm. But wait ...
Look! A fox is lying in the bush. The fox
is looking at the bird.

The fox runs after the bird, but it is
too slow. He cannot reach the fast bird.
The bird flies to the wood. Just in time.

9

It is a deep, dark wood. But wait ...
Look out! A stag is standing by the tree.
It is time to fly home.

The bird flies out of the wood, past
the farm, into the garden and into
the house. The granny is waiting there.

The bird is back home. Just in time.
He flies in and sits on the perch. There is
no stag, no fox, no dog, no cat. It is safe.

The granny is looking at the bird.
She shuts him safe inside. The bird
likes her. It is good to be home.

13

Bird's day out

Ideas for reading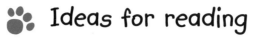

Written by Linda Pagett B.Ed(Hons), M.Ed
Lecturer and Educational Consultant

Learning objectives: identify the constituent parts of two-syllable words to support application of phonic knowledge and skills; make predictions showing an understanding of ideas and characters; tell stories and describe incidents from their own lives; interpret a text by reading aloud with some variety in pace and emphasis

Curriculum links: Citizenship

Fast words: two, like

Focus phonemes: ir (bird), ow (window), al, y, ea

Word count: 298

Getting started

- Revise the focus phonemes using flash cards. Write the word *bird* on the whiteboard and ask children to practise segmenting and blending the three phonemes that make it, e.g. *b-ir-d.*

- Read the title together and ask children what they understand by *A Day Out.* Ask them to give examples of days out they have been on.

- Look at the picture on the front cover and ask children what kind of bird is pictured. Prompt children to share what they know about parrots, e.g. *Where do we usually find parrots? Have you ever seen a parrot before? Where did you see it?*

- Read the blurb on the back cover together. Ask children to predict what will happen in the story.

Reading and responding

- Read pp2–3 aloud to the children, demonstrating how to read the exclamation marks with expression.

- Challenge children to find longer words, made up of more than one known part, e.g. granny, sleeping, looking. Ask them to clap the beats to these words. Explain that lots of words share the same endings, e.g. ing, and that recognising these helps us to read quickly.

- Encourage children to continue reading to p13. Support them as they read, helping them to tackle longer words and fast words.